MY HAIRY HALLOWEEN

Peculiar Mysteries & Romances

RENEE GEORGE

Barkside of the Moon Press

PARANORMAL MYSTERIES & ROMANCES

By Renee George

Peculiar Mysteries & Romances

Nora Black Midlife Psychic Mysteries

Age of Inno-Scents (Book 6)
Aroma Holiday (Book 7)

Witchin' Impossible Paranormal Mysteries

Witchin' Impossible (Book 1)
Rogue Coven (Book 2)
Familiar Protocol (Booke 3)
Mr & Mrs. Shift (Book 4)

Barkside of the Moon Paranormal Mysteries

Pit Perfect Murder (Book 1)
Murder & The Money Pit (Book 2)
The Pit List Murders (Book 3)
Pit & Miss Murder (Book 4)
The Prune Pit Murder (Book 5)
Two Pits and A Little Murder (Book 6)
Pits and Pieces of Murder (Book 7)

Grimoires of a Middle-aged Witch

Earth Spells Are Easy (Book 1)
Spell On Fire (Book 2)
When the Spells Blows (Book 3)
Spell Over Troubled Water (Book 4)
Ghost in the Spell (Book 5)

Hex Drive

Hex Me, Baby, One More Time (Book 1)
Oops, I Hexed It Again (Book 2)
I Want Your Hex (Book 3)
Hex Me With Your Best Shot (Book 4)

Hex Me All Night Long (Book 5)

Madder Than Hell

Gone With The Minion (Book 1)

Devil On A Hot Tin Roof (Book 2)

A Street Car Named Demonic (Book 3)

ACKNOWLEDGMENTS

I have to thank Michele Bardsley, my sister Robbin, and all the fans of this Peculiar series. You guys keep me wanting to write more and more in this world. May we be together for many mysteries to come. I love you. <3

And coffee. I can't forget to thank coffee.

BLURB

A Halloween bash, a high-risk pregnancy, and a vengeful prankster - just another "Peculiar" adventure for Sunny and her friends.

*****

It's celebration time in our small town, and I want to enjoy myself, but I am five months pregnant, which in therianthrope terms means this baby is spreading my ribs wide open and threatening to kick my liver right out my butt. Topping that, my psychic ability, which has been on the fritz is all revved up and in go, go, go mode.

I'm getting psychic visions of classic horror monsters getting stalked by the invisible man. With each new incident, his actions are getting more deadly.

I am only sure of one thing: Someone will die tonight if I don't figure out who the Wolfman is and how to stop the invisible man from killing him.

To my sisters and my brother.
You all make my life a little more peculiar in such a great way.

CHAPTER ONE

All Hallow's Eve...
Glowing Jack-O-Lanterns with gaping maws and jolly gazes were staggered between hay bales inside Delbert and Elbert Johnson's barn. The twin opossum shifters, decked out in patchy overalls, scarecrow face paint, and straw sticking out everywhere, had gone all out on the town's annual Halloween Bash from cobwebs in every corner to dry ice filled cauldrons overflowing with smoky white mist. Halloween music played over speakers. Swinging skeletons, the scent of nutmeg and cinnamon, and the occasional shrieks and moans emitting from a sound machine, frankly, was giving me a headache.

I scanned the crowd of townsfolk from my fortune teller booth, Chavvah's idea to keep me off my feet. I wanted to enjoy myself, but I was five months pregnant, which in therianthrope terms meant this baby was spreading my ribs wide open and threatening to kick my liver right out my butt.

1

In other words, I was less than a month from my due date.

Topping that, my psychic ability, which had been on the fritz since my first pregnancy with my son Jude, was all revved up and in *go, go, go* mode.

But nothing in Peculiar is ever as simple as it appears, and nothing about my psychic ability is ever easy. I was only sure of one thing, someone would die tonight if I didn't figure out who the Wolfman was *and* why the invisible man wanted him or her dead.

FOUR DAYS BEFORE HALLOWEEN...

I fluffed the large white sheet Chavvah, my BFF and sister-in-law, had delivered to me from our pal Ruth Thompson. Ruth had cut the queen-sized cotton into a circle, hemmed the edges down, created sleeves, and cut in eyes and a mouth hole.

"I can't go as a ghost," I whined. Baby Jude, nine months old now, crawled under my hem and wrapped his legs and arms around my leg. I walked forward on a stiff leg. He giggled, triggering all my mommy endorphins.

Chavvah, who I always thought was destined for greater things, had a life-changing summer. She'd fought psychotic killers, found out she could change into a wolf, and she was inhabited by a ginormous spirit named Brother Wolf. On top of that, she'd finally found the love of her life, Billy Bob Smith. They'd been in love with each other for a long time before they'd finally admitted it. I'd had a hard time observing and not interfering, because I'm impatient. Still, it hadn't been my affair. Alas, love happened on its own timeline.

"That costume is ridiculous, Sunny." Chav stood up straight, placing two determined fists on her hips. "You can't even tell who you are under all that."

"That's the point," I said.

Chav stomped her foot in irritation. She'd been so damaged by a kidnapping a year and a half ago that had left her with a terrible limp and residual pain, it was nice to see her moving so well. Becoming Billy Bob's mate and practicing spirit talking had almost healed her completely. Granted, her parents were still freaked out about her ability to shift into both a coyote and a wolf. Even my Babe had his qualms. Coyote shifters considered werewolves dangerous and unpredictable. I'd only known the one, and the doc was a sweetheart in my book. But old prejudices are hard to break. Even so, Babe liked Billy Bob a lot better now that he knew Billy Bob wasn't trying to steal me away.

As if.

"Oh, Sunny." Chav sighed. "Why didn't you just have Ruth cut a hole and make a collar so you could have your head out?"

Her question snapped me out of my parental euphoria. "My face looks like someone's been drilling for oil!"

I'd like to say that the second pregnancy was easier than the first, but I'd be a big, fat, liar liar pants on fire. I never knew how bad bad could get. I threw up morning, noon, and night for the first two months and still gained

3

weight. After that, I broke out in hives between my thighs that rubbed together every time I walked, and now I'd moved into the really unattractive last month, and it was taking its toll on my skin. I'd developed acne that had my cheeks red, bumpy, and inflamed. It was as if my body had been taken over by an alien. A rude, disgusting, smelly, farty, belchy, rashy, acidy-refluxy, someone-needs-to-kill-its-ass alien.

"I'm hideous. I don't want anyone to see me." Hence, the reason for the ghost costume with the full-face hoodie I'd asked Ruth to make me.

"But you're adorable," Chav said. She wiggled her fingers and raised her brows. "And scary."

"Boo." *Brrrrrrrrzzt.* "Oh, God."

"What was that?" Chavvah asked.

I struggled to get the ghost costume over my head, but the sleeves caught under my armpits. "Help me!" *Brrrrrrrrrzzzt.* "I'm suffocating."

Chav grabbed the back of my outfit and pulled it up and over my head. Breathing hard, I bent over and pulled Jude into my arms and collapsed onto the couch. *Brrzt. Squeak.*

Jude giggled.

"Not funny," I warned him.

He stuck his hand in my mouth in response and giggled again.

"Sunny, you know you're not supposed to be lifting. Anything. That includes my adorable nephew." She squeezed Jude's cheeks. "That's why I'm here."

Between Ruth, Chavvah, and Babe, I hadn't had a

moment to myself since Billy Bob diagnosed me with preeclampsia.

"He's small. It shouldn't count."

Therianthropes didn't develop as quickly as humans, so even though Jude was nine months old, his developmental stage was that of a five-month-old. Billy Bob told me his growth and maturity would be a little behind what I expected, but I wouldn't see a real slow down in his aging until after he was in his twenties. It seemed to be the point where their genetics kicked in and kept them looking young even into their sixties and seventies. Therianthropes could live up to two hundred years. A fact that I tried not to think about too often. I didn't want to confront the idea that I was aging more than twice as fast as my husband.

"It counts," Chav said. She took Jude from me and swung him around. His laughter brightened my dark mood.

Brrrrrsssss. No, God. Not a hisser. Those were the worst.

"Jesus, Sunny." Chav took three giant strides back, clutching Jude to her chest like a shield. "You're producing enough methane to power a small city."

"You're mean."

"Mean would be running out of the house before some faulty electrical wiring causes a spark and your gas blows us all the way back to California."

Chavvah was a born Missourian, but we had met in San Diego at a community college. We were both non-traditional students and bonded quickly.

"Mean and hateful," I muttered, but she wasn't wrong.

"You okay?" Chav asked.

5

I scowled at her shiny chestnut brown hair, flawless skin, and perfectly waxed brows. "My boobs are sweating." I was in a Triple D nursing bra that offered very little support, which meant my breasts mashed right up against my beach ball-sized belly.

"Your windows are open, and it's sixty-four degrees in the house."

I glared at Chav. Usually, her presence comforted me, but today, not so much. "I'm not going to the stupid Halloween party this weekend."

"Aww, Sunny. Don't be like that. You have to go. The whole town has been asking about you."

"That's an exaggeration." I'd taken the past two weeks off from work at Sunny's Outlook, the restaurant Chav and I owned together. My doctor, who also happened to be the future Mr. Chavvah Trimmel (kidding, I'm certain Billy Bob is keeping his last name. He seems progressive that way), said that my blood pressure and sugar levels had been a little too high on my previous visit. He'd finally given me the "okay" for brief activity, which meant, technically I could go to the big Halloween bash, but really, did I want to be farting all night in a room full of shifters and their super sensitive noses?

No, I did not.

"I'm just going to stay in and watch vintage scary movies." The old black and whites were so much scarier than modern day horror. Chavvah had been over every night for the past week, and we'd already viewed *The Wolfman*, *The Mummy*, *The Mummy II*, *Frankenstein*, *The Bride of Frankenstein*, and *The Creature from the Black Lagoon*.

"At least the invisible man won't complain about my abnormal bodily discharges."

"Just because you can't see him holding his breath, doesn't mean it's not happening."

I threw a throw pillow at Chav, careful to aim at her knees and not hit Jude. "Give me my baby and get out."

"I'm making you dinner."

"Get to the kitchen." My lower lip jutted of its own accord.

"You know, watching all those horror flicks is probably the reason you're having weird dreams."

"I had another one last night."

"Not about invisible men nailing vampire coffins shut again, I hope."

I shook my head. "This time the invisible man took a crap on the Bride of Frankenstein's carriage. It was pretty gross."

"Why would he want to do that?"

"Because he was jealous, angry, and tired of not being seen."

"That's very specific," Chav said.

"It was a very specific dream."

"I'm going to put Jude in his play pen, so you're not tempted to pick him up again. Lay off the Lon Chaney for a couple of days," she scolded then went around the corner to the kitchen.

"Yes, mother." I looked at my phone. "It's after five. Babe should be home soon. What are you fixing for dinner?"

I wadded the ghost costume up and threw it on my

bed. Chavvah spoke loud enough for me to hear her from the other room. "I found this great recipe for vegetarian lasagna. It has generous layers of chunky vegetables, spicy red sauce, ricotta cheese, cottage cheese, and mozzarella cheese. I'm finishing it off with a toasted pumpkin seed topping. It's high in protein and low in salt, but still delicious."

"Great." No salt. Ugh. It was part of my new diet thanks to the high blood pressure. I heard the can opener churning. "It's so sweet of you to cook for me, Chav. You really don't have to you know? Babe's not a bad cook."

"Babe can make eggs and grits. You need more than that for a healthy baby."

Chavvah had been worried about me since Billy Bob put me on bed rest. "You know I'm okay, right?" I walked into the kitchen.

Chav stood at the counter dicing carrots, broccoli, and cauliflower (or what I liked to call fuel for my farts). I took a seat at our new dining room table. It was bar height with tall high back chairs. The table top was a combination of darker and lighter woods. I really liked that I didn't have to squat to sit in a chair. Even more, I liked that it wasn't the same table and chairs that I'd been tied to when Randall Lowry, a psycho who'd thought Chav was his destiny, had held me hostage to get to her.

Randall, who'd been born without the ability to shift into animal form, had believed sacrificing my BFF would give him skin walker abilities. His twin brother Chance, who could shift, had been aiding him for years. We found out later that they'd skinned and murdered more than two dozen therianthropes in a four-year period. I still don't know how they got away with such atrocities for so long.

"Just because it's nearly under control doesn't mean you're out of the woods, chick. You've got to keep the diet going. High protein. No salt."

I waved at her. "Yeah, yeah. You meeting up with our hunky doc tonight?"

Chav smiled, a healthy blush rising in her cheeks. "He wants me to come by his place for some dessert he's making."

"Or eating." I grinned. The baby in my belly kicked. I peed. "Freaking hell." I grabbed my belly and silently scolded Junior.

"Serves you right." Chav laughed.

"Hey, Willy Boden is coming down in a couple of days for the Halloween shindig."

Willy, a fiery, red-headed, freckle-faced bobcat shifter, was the lead security officer for the Tri-State Council. Chav and I had gotten to know her during the TSC Jubilee that Peculiar had hosted in June. The same Jubilee that had brought two serial killers to our town. I'd initially thought she was a cougar since her brother represented the Felidae, or big cats, on the council. Bobcats weren't that large. They actually looked like oversized domestic cats with wicked cool ears and a bobbed tail. Hence the name.

"Yeah? How come Willy's coming to visit?"

"Maybe because we're kick ass women, and everyone wants to be our friend." Though it had been several months since I'd been able to lift my leg up high enough to even reach an ass.

"True story," Chav said. "We are pretty tough."

"And adorable," I amended.

Chav smiled. "Well, you are, anyhow." She scooped up the diced veggies and began to sauté them in a hot pan with a little olive oil and minced garlic. The smell had my mouth watering. "It'll be good to see her."

The front door opened, and I heard the familiar footfalls of my hot, hunky husband, Babel Trimmel. "Hey, darling. Where you at?" he hollered from the door.

"In the kitchen," I said. I didn't have to holler. Babe and Chavvah were both coyote shifters so they could hear me drop a pin from across the room.

"Sorry, I'm late. That damn Evelyn Meyers kept me in a meeting over her beef with Sheriff Taylor," he said when he came around the corner. He looked startled when he saw me. "Why are you sitting around in your bra and underwear?"

"Because I'm hot," I said, grabbing a napkin and sopping up boob sweat.

"And gassy," Chavvah added helpfully. Not.

I glared at her. Babe dipped down and kissed me. His soft lips made my whole body tingle. He'd grown his hair out a little, and his brown hair fell down over his bright blue eyes. He smiled. "You're beautiful."

"You knocked me up. You have to say that."

He kissed me again, this time, very convincingly, and more than my body tingled.

"You guys are gross," Chavvah said.

"Why is Evelyn mad at the sheriff now?" I asked,

ignoring my BFF's protest against PDA. "Other than he married her sister."

Evelyn was Jean Taylor's sister. They'd fallen out over Sheriff Taylor thirty years ago. Apparently, the elder sister had designs on the up and coming lawman in town, but he only had eyes for Jean. Boy, that Evelyn sure knew how to carry a grudge. I didn't have the energy to hate anyone that hard.

"Apparently we have a prankster in town."

"Pranks?" Chavvah gave me a pointed look. "Like when someone sucks all the jelly out of your donuts and puts them back in the box?"

"What?" I rubbed my belly. "The baby made me do it."

Babe rubbed my shoulder. "That's your story, and you're sticking to it."

"Damn straight."

My gorgeous husband laughed, and it was a delicious sound. "It wasn't quite so harmless. Evelyn's prankster smeared a stinky slime all over her car, and she swears Sheriff Taylor is responsible."

"She'd find a way to blame the clouds on that man if she could." Chav put the pan of food inside the oven. "That woman is a menace."

That was no lie. "If the sheriff didn't do it, who did?"

"You're too pregnant for crime fighting," Chav said.

"I'm going to change." Babe kissed my temple. "Be right back."

Chav gave her brother a quick hug before he left the room. "I have to go too."

"Oooooo. Are you in a hurry to massage the old spirit stick with Billy Bob?" I asked just to watch her blush.

"Stop it."

I wiggled my brows. "Going to sweat out those demons?"

"You're not funny."

"Are you planning on worshipping at the totem pole?"

Chavah put her hands on both her hips, leaned down to me and asked, "Jealous?"

"A little." We both laughed. The diagnosis of preeclampsia had meant no sex. At all. Which sucked because, well, I wanted to strip off my husband's clothes and boink him every time he was near me.

Speaking of sexy, he walked back into the kitchen wearing blue sweat pants and a gray T-shirt that hugged his massive chest. I must have had a boinking look on my face because Chav turned to her brother to divert sexy-time to food. "Lasagna is in. Babe, take it out in forty-five minutes. Salad's in the fridge."

"Thanks," I told her. "I appreciate all your help."

I wouldn't have made it the past couple weeks without her pitching in. I'd hated feeling like an invalid, but spending a lot of time with Chavvah had made it worth it. I didn't begrudge her happiness, not one iota. She and Billy Bob couldn't be more perfect together. Especially with him being a shaman and her being a spirit talker. But it also meant that we saw less and less of each other outside of work. I'd began to really miss her.

"I hope you change your mind about the Halloween party," she said. "How about going as a fortune teller?"

"Ha ha."

"I'm serious. You can wear loose, colorful clothes, a scarf on your head, maybe a whacky wig. It'll be fun."

"I'll think about it."

She patted me on the shoulder. The color in the room drained, everything including Chavvah and Babe went gray, and then...

...The scene is right out of The Mummy. The mummy is covered in bandages a contrast to his gray skin and dark eyes. He is surrounded by fierce Egyptian warriors, exotic women, and an archeologist.

The archeologist steps between the mummy and an Egyptian princess. He shouts, "She deserves better than you!"

"Mind your own business," the mummy says with an Ozark accent that is very unMummy-like.

The archeologist shoves him. The mummy counters with a punch to the archeologist's jaw.

A woman screams, "Stop it, both of you."

The mummy's eyes flash with anger. "You're a worthless piece of shit." He grabs his princess by the wrist and begins to drag her away.

Suddenly, I'm no longer outside the scene. I am in it, watching.

No one notices. The archeologist is right. The mummy doesn't deserve his princess. She is too good for him. Too good for the archeologist, too. When the mummy walks right past me with the princess in tow, neither of them even acknowledged my presence, and a seething anger takes root inside me.

I looked down at my body, it is flat. No boobs or belly. I wore a light trench coat, dark trousers, and black dress shoes. I hold out my hands. There is nothing. They, like me, are invisible. Unseen. I need to be seen.

So I give the mummy a little push. The monster loses his balance and falls into a hole. He falls and falls. I am tired of being invisible. They won't ignore me anymore. I'll make sure of it.

"Sunny. Sunny!"

My eyes flickered open. I gasped for breath.

Babe stared at me, his green eyes tensed with worry. "What happened?"

"I'm calling Billy Bob," Chavvah said.

"No. Don't." I was still in the dining room chair. I couldn't shake the feeling of being so alone and invisible. "It was just another bad dream."

"You were wide awake, Sunny. I've seen you go into one of your trances when you have a vision."

"Well, unless The Mummy and the Invisible Man have moved to Peculiar, I think it's safe to say that was no vision." I rubbed my belly. "Pregnancy brain, I'm sure."

CHAPTER TWO

Three days until the Halloween party...
      The next morning I drove into town for a few personal items. At this point, I was looking for a change of scenery. Two weeks of staring at the inside walls of my house had me a little stir crazy. It was probably the reason I'd had the daymare about monsters. Ruth's oldest daughter Dakota had come over to watch Jude for me, which meant for a couple glorious hours, I was absolutely free.

It was unseasonably warm, and I planned to enjoy the good weather while it lasted. I hated Missouri winters, almost as much as they hated me. Two words. Winter itch. Yeah, it's a thing. Dry, flaky, itchy skin brought on by cold weather and dry indoor heat. I never had this problem when I lived in Southern California. But, I also didn't have Babe, my child, my best friend, and a community of good people, well, therianthropes. Other than the great weather, my life had been crap there.

Birds were in V-formation, flying south for the winter as I pulled into the handicap parking space outside the Johnson's General Store. Since therians were rarely disabled for any amount of time, I wasn't taking the space from someone who needed it. Besides, the doc insisted that even though I was off bed rest, I still needed to take it easy.

The store was located directly across from Sunny's Outlook, the restaurant that Chavvah and I owned together. It was a Monday, and lunch was in full swing. I'd stop over later when it calmed down.

I waddled inside the store. It was old-fashioned with real hardwood floors and four rows about fifteen feet long. The walls on either side were covered in shelves that went from floor to ceiling. The twins kept a step ladder handy for items that needed to be pulled down from the shelf. It always smelled like wood polish and rubbing alcohol in here, but I liked it.

"Hey, Sunny," Delbert Johnson said. While he restocked shampoos and conditioners, his twin, Elbert, worked the cash register. Delbert grabbed two more bottles from an open box at his feet. "Land sake's woman, you're resembling Pop-n-Fresh oven biscuits."

"And you resemble Santa Claus," I said. "But in a month or two, I'll look like my old self again, and you'll be getting fitted for the red suit."

Elbert, at the back of the store, laughed so hard he snorted. "What can we do for you today, Sunny?"

"The hemorrhoid medicine is over on the far wall," Delbert said with a twinkle of mischief.

"Ha ha." As it happened, I did need some butt luggage medicine, but there was no way in hell I'd get it from the Johnson twins now. I'd rather order it from Wonderzin.-com. Or make Chavvah buy it for me. "I'm assuming it's next to the adult diapers. That's why you're so familiar with the location."

Delbert laughed. He walked over to me. "You look great, kid. Are you doing okay?"

"Other than the second coming of puberty," and a whole slew of really gross body stuff, "I'm doing splendid."

Elbert joined us out on the store floor. "We heard you had to be off your feet for a couple of weeks. You sure you should be out and about now?"

Even though the twins looked alike, Delbert had a slimmer face and Elbert had a small freckle by his eye. However, the worry on their faces was identical. "I really am good," I assured them. "Billy Bob gave me the thumbs up to get out of bed. As long as I'm not overdoing it, I'll be fine."

Delbert put his hand on my shoulder. "Well, we have a brand-new wheelbarrow we can lend Babe if you need to be pushed around."

"Like a feed sack," Elbert added, a sly grin crinkling the corner of his eyes.

"You both should take the act on the road, but until then, I need some pimple cream."

"For your butt?"

I glared at Delbert. "You have an unhealthy obsession with my ass."

The door jingled and opened. Mark Smart, the local

mortician and a wereopossum like the Johnsons walked inside. "Nice day," he said to all of us.

"Morning, Mark." I smiled. Mark owned Smart and Son Funeral Home. He was also the elected coroner for Peculiar.

"Morning, Mrs. Trimmel." He smiled, his white teeth gleaming brighter than his white hair. Typical characteristics for opossums. "You are looking well."

"I look like a giant ham," I told him. "But I appreciate the lie. How's Jackson doing?"

"Okay. You know how boys are."

I didn't actually, but as Jude got older, I was sure going to find out. "Staying out of trouble I hope."

"Yes, Ma'am. Jackson's a good kid. He was accepted to Southwest University in the fall."

"Oh yeah, what's he studying."

"Science, believe it or not. My kid's got a head for numbers and formulas and such."

I knew Mark wanted to pass his business down to Jackson. I was both happy and sad for him. "It's great seeing you. And I'm thrilled for Jackson."

"Sunny." Elbert had walked the next aisle over and brought me some maximum strength acne meds. "I'll put it on the mayor's tab."

"Thanks, El." I gave his beard a quick crinkle then I wagged my finger at Delbert. "I'll see you both later."

The baby kicked, I farted, and truthfully, I peed myself a little. Both opossum shifters turned red before they both burst out giggling.

"I hate you both."

With as much indignation I could muster, I turned on my heel and stormed out. Their raucous laughter followed behind me, and I didn't need super-shifter ears to hear them even after the door closed behind me.

"Sunny!" I heard someone call. I looked up and saw Evelyn Meyers running across the road from Sunny's Outlook. I groaned. Babe told me she was angry because Sheriff Taylor had cited her for a street violation for parking in front of her store, Banded Collectables and Antiques. She'd only recently opened the store and had a truck deliver a bunch of inventory in a no loading zone. Unfortunately, it was wider than the parking space and encroached on the road.

I personally think that if she hadn't been the Sheriff's sister-in-law, he would have let it go with a warning. From what I'd heard from Ruth, Jean and Evelyn had a falling out years ago, and Evelyn took every opportunity to point out Jean's flaws to her.

I plastered a wide smile on my face and forced it to my eyes. "Hi, Evelyn."

She gave me an assessing look. "You are getting... round," she said.

I wondered if Sheriff Taylor could give her a ticket for being a jerk. "Back at you," I said then added as if it were a mistake, "I mean, you're looking healthy today. What can I do for you?"

"Your husband is avoiding me, and I want him to take care of the police problem in this town."

"Babel can't tell the Sheriff how to do his job."

She scoffed. "He can so. According to his job description, his duties put him in charge of all forms of town government, including the police, the fire department, and so on. If he wants to keep his job, he'll take me seriously."

My ears burned as a slow simmer of anger bubbled up in me. "Are you threatening my husband?" I asked with the quiet calm of a serial killer.

Evelyn opened her mouth. She closed it. Then opened it again. "I should have known I'd get no help from an outsider. Good day, Ms. Haddock."

"Mrs. Trimmel," I corrected her, but she was already walking away. Bitch. If I hadn't been ordered to avoid strenuous activity, I would have tackled her to the ground and shoved my fist right into her snootiness. Well, probably not, but the thought made me feel better.

I ran into Sally Michaels and her daughter Miriam on my way to Dolly's Beauty Shop. Sally was a coyote shifter like my Babe. She and her daughter were tall with long legs and narrow hips. Sally was a blonde, while Miriam took after her father and had darker almost cinnamon colored locks. Like Babe and Chav, they had angular faces and sharp, straight noses. Sally owned the dress shop, The Formal Invitation. She'd done a beautiful job on my wedding dress in February, but I don't think she'd forgiven me for ruining her creation before the whole town had gotten a glimpse.

Across the road on the courthouse lawn, an excavator squealed and roared to life. A large area was cordoned off where they'd been digging the day before. A water pipe had cracked open, and the water department had patched it. Babe had told me they'd be closing it in today.

"Hi, Dolly. Miriam," I yelled to get over the noise and cupped my hands under my belly out of habit. "You having a mother-daughter day." I smiled, feeling wistful. I couldn't wait until I had a girl to shop for.

The excavator grew louder. Miriam, who was seventeen now, snorted. "Not."

Dolly gave her daughter a hard stare, then softened her expression when she looked back to me. "We're meeting Paul," that was her husband, "down at the Outlook for lunch."

Oh, customers. Yay. "Don't let me stop you then!" Of course, the work stopped across the street, and a loud, angry conversation drew our attention.

Kyle Avery, the young punk and recent high school graduate who had been partially responsible for my failed wedding pushed his best friend, Roger Parks. "Take it back!" he said.

A small crowd, including Michele Thompson, Karina Wells, Jackson Smart, Brandon Messer and his sister Selena, stood around them. An elderly man I didn't know, but I had seen around town before stood behind the group. I raised my brow.

"Or you'll what?" Roger asked. I did not want to intervene. Those two boys could beat each other to a pulp for all I cared, but I was a parent now, and I had an overly developed sense of responsibility.

"She deserves better than you," Kyle said.

"Mind your own business," Roger said.

Karina Wells yelled, "Stop it, both of you!"

Kyle shoved Roger. Roger punched Kyle.

I felt woozy with a strong sense of *deja vu*.

"Hey!" Taylor Thompson walked out of the courthouse. "Take it somewhere else!" He usually wasn't so direct, not like his twin Tyler, but seeing his sister must have caused his reaction.

He and Tyler were both tall and blond, but Taylor was slimmer than his brother, and unlike the Johnson twins, Tyler and Taylor were complete opposites. Tyler was right handed. Taylor was left. Tyler was aggressive. Taylor was diplomatic. And so on. Taylor's temperament is the reason Babe had hired him as the human resource manager for the city positions. That and his degree in business management.

Every one of the teenagers stared at him as if he'd turned purple and sprouted horns.

Taylor Thompson gestured to his younger sister. "Michele," he said. "Get over here."

She separated herself from the group.

When Roger grabbed Karina by the arm and tried to pull her away, I dazedly walked right out into traffic. A blaring horn startled me. I yelped and stumbled sideways as Brady Corman, a coyote shifter and the ex-mayor of Peculiar, stared at me from behind the wheel of his black pickup truck.

He got out and ran to me. "Are you all right? What were you thinking just walking out into the road like that?"

Brady was a good man, even if he hadn't acted like it for a few years. His son Jo Jo was one of my first friends in town, and he worked for Chav and me at Sunny's outlook. Brady lost his wife, the love of his life ten years ago, and instead of focusing on raising his son, he'd concentrated on the bottom of a bottle. He'd finally pulled his act together, but he and Jo Jo's relationship was a work in progress. I felt sorry for him most of the time, but it didn't stop me from getting irritated when he snapped at me.

"You watch your tone, Brady."

His face reddened, but a cry for help redirected our attention. We both turned toward the courthouse. Karina Wells sobbed. "Someone help him." The group that had surrounded the earlier fight were scattered and chaotic. Taylor Thompson was ordering the men on the dozer and the excavator to stop.

"Help me," I told Brady. "Help me get over there."

"You need to sit down."

"No," I told him. "I need to know what's happened."

"Babe is going to kill me if anything bad happens to you."

"Brady! Don't argue with a pregnant woman."

Brady put his arm around me, and we walked the rest of the way across the street. Brandon Messer and his sister were closest.

"What's happened?" I asked Selena since I knew her better than her older brother.

"Roger fell in the hole over there. He's not moving." She covered her mouth. "He looked so awful."

Soon Deputy Farraday and Connelly were on the scene. Thompson must have called them. They were moving everyone back from the scene. Eldin Farraday, a slender gray fox shifter with gray-green eyes, put barricade tape up in front of me.

I touched his arm. "Is Roger okay?"

"I think he might have broken his leg is all, but we don't want to move him until the doc gets here."

Two arms wrapped around me from behind. I looked over at Brady, who stood a few feet away, then turned my head to the man behind me. "Babe," I said.

"You okay?" he asked.

"The Mummy," I told him. "Someone pushed The Mummy into the well."

CHAPTER THREE

*L*ater in the evening, I lounged on my couch, unable to shake the feeling that I should have done something to stop the fight before Roger ended up hurt. Yes, the kid was a grade-A ass, but he was someone's son. Now that I had a son of my own, it meant something to me.

Doctor Shaman Billy Bob Smith, who stood at six-feet four inches, knelt next to me, stethoscope hanging out of his ears as he pumped the volume up on the blood pressure cuff cutting off the circulation to my bicep. His silvery-gray eyes swirled with concentration as he let out the air slowly.

"Well?" I asked.

His full mouth thinned with irritation. Gosh, he really had the most beautiful skin. It was the color of café au lait and no doubt, was just as delicious. My girl Chav was a lucky, lucky woman. And, since I'd accidentally saw him naked early in the summer, I knew she was lucky in other ways as well. Hubba. Hubba. I dropped my gaze. Sheesh.

Slobbering over my best friend's mate was so not cool. Especially since my own mate was covered in awesome sauce. Or gravy. *Gravy.* I could really use some gravy. I started to drool.

Literally.

I rubbed my mouth.

"Sunny?" Babe brought me a cold iced herbal tea and set it down on the end table. When he bent over, I couldn't take my eyes off his rutti tutti booty. Rawr.

When Billy Bob stood up, Chavvah came over, dipped her face to my ear and said, "Greedy."

"I'd have to be blind, doll." I smiled. "There is some generous eye candy in this room, and you know mamma's got a sweet tooth."

Chav and I giggled. Then she said, "Ew. That's my brother you're talking about over there."

"He's not my brother." I wiggled my eyes at Babe when he met my gaze.

Babe put his hand on Billy Bob's shoulder. "I think she's feeling better, Doc."

"I heard," he said. His grin made me blush. Damn shifters and their damn bionic hearing. "Sunny, your BP is a little high. I think you better take it easy for a couple more days. The excitement today was too much. I told you to take it easy."

"If I take it any easier, I'm going to be comatose," I grumbled.

"I'll make sure she stays in bed," Babe said.

"None of that, either." Billy Bob raised his brow at me. "I mean it. You've already had one premature delivery. Unless you want another, you'll follow doctor's orders."

"Yes, sir." I gave him a three finger salute. I really wanted to give him a one finger salute, but I didn't.

I heard Chav say, "You are sexy as hell when you're bossy."

"Hey!" I turned in time to see her kissing him like she was going to eat him. "Take it to your own place. This home is for monks and celibates. If I can't get any here, than neither can you." Traitor.

Chav disengaged from her man, walked across the room to me, kissed my forehead. "Love you, babe. But I got my own bed rest to tend to."

Billy Bob laughed. "Doctor's orders."

I stuck my tongue out at both of them.

After they left, Babe scooped me up from the couch. I felt like a giddy school girl as he carried me as if I weighed a couple of ounces, not one-hundred and eighty-five pounds. "You are the man," I said breathlessly against his neck. Pleasure filled me as goosebumps arose on his skin.

"Now, Sunny." He set me down on the bed and smoothed my hair away from my face. "If I had the green light...the things I would do to you."

"Tell me about it." This could be our very own version of phone sex. Yay!

"Nope."

Bummer.

"I don't know if I could keep my hands off you. Why don't you tell me why you tried to get in the middle of a fight on the courthouse lawn today?"

Uh oh. Here came the lecture. Crap. "Technically, I went over there after the fight was over."

"Well, Roger is lucky he didn't get more than a broken leg. Horsing around a work site could've ended with him having a broken neck.."

"Next thing you know, you'll be calling them pesky kids and telling them to turn their music down."

Babe grimaced. "I'm not becoming that guy."

I put my index and my thumb an inch apart and said, "Pretty close."

He snarled, and man, it just made him sexier.

"Stop that. You know I like it when you go all growly."

He smiled then. "Okay. I forgive you."

Babe kissed me, and I melted into his arms. The baby inside me moved. Babe made a pleased noise, almost like a purr. There was nothing quite so proud as a procreating therian.

I sighed, thinking about my daydream and how similar it had been to what happened to Roger Parks. "Someone pushed him into that hole, Babe."

"Did you see it happen?"

"Sorta. It matched my vision."

"You mean the one where The Mummy fights the villagers for his bride?" He gave me a sympathetic look. "You're pregnant, Sunny. You know that messes with your gift."

"The fight played out just like I saw it, words and all. Only it happened between Kyle and Roger."

"There were a half dozen or more witnesses. No one saw anyone else push Roger into that hole. He's an arrogant ass who was too angry to watch where he was walking."

Put out with my husband for at least not making even a slight effort to, believe me, I snuggled against a large pillow. "Hand me Jude."

Babel brought me our son. I cuddled him close and kissed his tiny fingers. "It was a psychic vision, Babe."

"You've been watching a lot of horror flicks this past week," he said. "It's no wonder you're having daymares about mummies and irate villagers."

Baby Jude stuck his chubby little fingers up my nose, and I pulled my head back. "Maybe." Though I knew in my bones, it was more than just hormones.

"Ruth sent me home with a peach pie. Do you want a piece?"

I glared at Babe. "You're just telling me now?"

"Is that a yes?"

"You bet your sweet bippy." I sat up in bed.

Jude said, "Mamamamamamama."

I kissed his cherubic little face. "You are sweeter than any pie," I told him. But when Babe brought me a plate with a generous portion of peach pie and a scoop of vanilla ice cream, my mouth began to water. It wasn't gravy. No, it was way better.

"You used to look at me like that," Babe teased.

"Maybe you should start wearing ice cream to bed," I said.

"Is that a request?"

I dragged my gaze away from dessert and up to my man. "Hell yes. As soon as the doc gave the A-Okay. But first…" I turned my attention back to the pie. I used my fork to scoop a little pie, making sure I got both crust and fruit on there, then added a little ice cream. I put the perfect bite into my mouth and *mmmm mmm*.

Oh no. Babe's vibrant blue eyes turned to a dull gray.

I must have had a strange look on my face because I heard Babe say, "Sunny. Sunny, are you all right?"

The world around me, once again, became grainy and black and white.

The swamp creature rose up from the murky depths of his oily home. It was actually super disgusting. It smelled like sulfur and poop. I watched him, so arrogant, the way he lauded his power over everyone. The way he looked at me was like I was a flea on a dog. I couldn't take it anymore. I wouldn't let another single creature walk all over me. I wasn't a doormat. I was a person. Flesh and blood. I would show them. Show them all.

I set a trap for the swamp man. I put a snake into his cesspit. When he screamed, I threw in a torch.

Kaboom!

That'll teach him. I'm not invisible. Not to him. Not anymore.

I blinked. Babe stared at me. "What did you see?"

"The swamp man catches on fire." I shook my head, trying to dam the tears. "It's the invisible man again. I can't see him, Babe. I can't."

CHAPTER FOUR

Two Days until Halloween...
Ruth Thompson came over at noon with lunch and Wilhelmina "Willy" Boden. Both were a welcome surprise. She relieved Dakota, who had just put Jude down for a nap.

"Bedrest sucks," I lamented.

"Are you kidding me?" Willy pulled a chair from the kitchen into the living room. "I'd give my eye-teeth for a couple of days off my feet. The Tri-State Council is a pain in my ass. The entire infrastructure has been reorganized, and they expect me to keep everyone safe, as long as I do it their way. That's not how I work. I'm about to tell them to take their job and--"

"Shove it," I finished for her.

"More like shove it up their ass," she said.

I smiled. I liked Willy. She was shorter than me, with more curves, unless I am super preggers, of course, grass green eyes, and had a thick head of wavy, almost carrot-orange hair. To top it off, she was sassy and honest, two things I admired in my friends.

Ruth, who did not have a potty mouth, was about to go apoplectic. I once heard her say GD, not the actual words, just the initials, and I thought the world was going to stop revolving on its axis. "I believe we need to get something in that mouth of yours," she said diplomatically. "Both of you."

Ruth, who was a deer shifter, had the beautiful features of a Disney princess. Turned up small nose, high, wide cheeks, pointed chin, full but narrow lips. Pretty much the human version of a deer. Or what I imagined elves and fairies might look like if they existed. She and her husband Ed own Doe Run automotive, and she was my second best friend ever. And it wasn't just because she always brought me pie.

Speaking of which... I spied a pie tin in her stack of food platters. "Is that pumpkin pie?"

"You know it," Ruth said.

"I really missed your cooking, Ruth," Willy said. She rubbed her fingers together. "So tell me all the gossip."

Ruth shook her head. "Well, as you can see, Sunny's pregnant."

"I knew that before I left," Willy said. "How's Chavvah and that big old hunka doctor? Have they tied the knot yet?"

"Not yet," I said. "They haven't even set a date." I had no idea what was preventing them from speaking vows, but I figured Chav and Billy Bob would get there in their own time. They were slow movers as evidenced by how long it took them to get together in the first place. "What about you? You seeing anyone?"

"Nope, not a soul," Willy said. "I have the worst taste in men. They either turn out to be undercover FBI agents or dead."

Ruth gasped. I snarfed. I mean, it was terrible that her ex-boyfriend ended up a victim of the skin peeling serial killers. I mean really awful. I don't know why I laughed.

I pointed to my belly when Ruth gave me an appalled look. "Hormones," I said. I circled my finger by my ear. "They're making me crazy."

"I wish I had such a good excuse," Willy lamented. "Chav dodged a bullet with Dom." Dom was the undercover FBI agent. He and Chav had gone out on a date before Billy Bob made his move. "He's a typical bear. All sweet and cuddly one minute and all roar the next."

"I don't know about you, but I always like a little roar with my cuddles."

Ruth laughed now. She dished me up a scoop of chickpea salad and put it on a plate with a black bean burger Chav made for me at Sunny's Outlook.

"Oh." Willy made a cringy face. "What is that smell?"

"Sorry." I waved my hand over my lap. It had been a silent but deadly. Tears crested my eyes. "I'm a farty-mcfartster. I can't control it."

"Damn, my eyes are watering," Willy said.

Tough audience. I laughed. "I missed you, chick."

"Back at you, girlfriend." She got up and moved her chair closer to the window. "I think I'll miss you from over here, though. No offense."

"Lots taken."

Ruth said, "Oh, did you hear about Smart Funeral home?"

A change of subject. Yay. "Tell us."

"Someone glued all the display coffin lids shut." She shook her head.

"You're kidding." It was just like my first nightmare. Holy crap. And poor Mark. Why would anyone have a vendetta against him? He was a decent man. He doubled as the coroner in town, though it was more a token position. Billy Bob, as the only medical doctor around, had the last say when it came to how someone died in Peculiar.

"No," Ruth said earnestly. "The glue ruined the finishes. He reported it to the sheriff." She grimaced. "I had just been there the day before for a funeral."

"I'm sorry. Did you lose someone close?"

She shook her head. "No. It was an elderly man from Silver Fox Senior Center. He didn't have any kin left. Mark called me and asked if I could get some mourners out for him." Her brown eyes swiveled up at me. "Don't be hurt. If you hadn't been on bedrest, you would have been my first call."

A knot eased in me. "I'm glad." I leaned in toward her. "I've *seen* these incidents."

"What do you mean?" Willy said. "How did you *see* them?"

"I was there when Roger fell," I said quickly. I forgot that Willy didn't know I was psychic. Even worse, she didn't know I was human. The town had voted and decided to keep that information from the Tri-Council. When in human form, you couldn't tell a human from a shifter, and since I spent all my time around therians, I certainly smelled like one.

Willy gave me a curious look, but Jude woke up from his noon nap and started fussing before she could ask any questions. "I'll get him." Willy followed the sounds to the baby's room.

When she left the room, Ruth's eyes widened, and she said in a quick whisper, "I like Willy, too, but you have to be careful. She still answers to the Tri-Council."

"I know," I whined. I couldn't believe I almost blew it. "Hormones." I was blaming a lot on this pregnancy. I hoped my baby girl had broad shoulders. "But I dreamed all of this, Ruth. From the coffins, to Evelyn's car, and Roger falling in the hole."

Willy came in swinging Jude in her arms. He laughed every time he flew in the air. He was such a happy baby. Easy too.

"Mamamamama," Jude said. He kept his eye on me, but he contented himself to letting Willy toss him around, especially since I couldn't. "So what did you see?" Willy asked.

I was saved by the bell, literally, because Ruth's phone rang.

"It's the sheriff's office," she said. "Must be Tyler."

Her son, Tyler Thompson was a deputy sheriff, the same as his identical twin Taylor who'd had been at the courthouse when Roger got hurt. I really like Taylor. I did not like Tyler. That young man had been coarse to me when I arrived in town. He had a beef with Babe's deceased brother Judah, and somehow, that animosity got displaced my way. He'd apologized, but I still didn't like him.

Ruth answered. "Hello." She looked mildly surprised. "What can I do for you, Eldin?"

Eldin Farraday was also a deputy. I immediately went on alert, especially as I watched Ruth's face drained of color. I sat up straight. "What is it?"

"I'll be right there," Ruth said. Her hands were shaking now. "Tyler's been rushed to Doctor Smith. He's got second degree burns, and they think maybe a concussion. They've called Darla. She and the girls are on their way out to the clinic now."

Darla was Tyler's wife. She and Tyler had twin girls, April and Mia.

"How did it happen?" I asked, worry lacing my tone.

"Something about an outhouse and a snake. A prank gone wrong, Eldin says."

A chill swept through me. "You said it got burned. So, there was a fire?"

Ruth gaped at me. "Did you...?"

I nodded. Willy glared at us suspiciously. "What are you two hiding?"

"Sunny needs to talk to the sheriff," Ruth said.

"I'm on bedrest," I told her. "I'm allowed to lounge, that's about it."

"I've got to get to the doc's. Willy, could you stay and help Sunny?"

"Sure, of course." She bounced Jude on her knee. "But I expect an explanation when this is over."

"You bet." Ruth grabbed her purse. "I'm calling Sheriff Taylor on the way. He can decide if he wants to come talk to you. But if you know anything about what happened to Tyler, you need to tell him."

"He'll think I'm crazy."

"He already thinks you're insane." She took my hand. "I know you and Tyler don't get along, but this is my boy. I love him, Sunny. Like you love Jude. Please help."

"Okay." What else could I say? Not much in front of Willy. Even if I could, though, the vision had been like the others. The invisible man did it. Of course, Tyler played the swamp man in my little creature feature. I was getting sick of my gift, which had always been unpredictable, being completely useless—and couching real events within the fictional confines of monster movies.

Ruth left, Willy went to change Jude's diaper, and I was left alone to think about my whacky classic horror visions.

Were all these incidents perpetrated by the same person? Or was my pregnancy visions just giving me a generic invisible bad guy each time? What if there were multiple pranksters? The incidents had definitely escalated from harmless and annoying to dangerous and injurious. I felt sure it had to be one person. But who?

I rubbed my hands together, held my breath and concentrated on the invisible man. *Psychic vision power activate!*

Nothing happened, of course. I let out the breath.

"Are you constipated?" Willy asked. I hadn't realized she'd come back in the room.

"Yes," I told her because a) I really was, and b) it was an

easier justification for my weird behavior. My phone rang. Saved by the bell again. "Hello."

"Sunny, this is Sheriff Taylor. Ruth told me to call you."

"She told you, huh?" I got a vision of Ruth ordering the sheriff around. "I can't come in. Not unless Billy Bob says it's okay."

"I know. I called Babe first. He told me a little bit about what's been going on with you. Can you talk?"

"Uhm, Willy Boden is in town visiting me." I tried to put a cheery note in my voice.

"Understand. I'm on my way to you so we can talk in private."

"Thanks." We hung up.

Willy stared at me suspiciously. "What the hell is going on?"

Willy was too smart for her own good. Or rather, my own good. I grimaced. "Ugh." I clutched my belly.

"Are you all right?"

I felt slightly guilty for using my pregnancy to misdirect Willy's attention. "Nausea," I said.

"Look, you rest. I'll take care of Jude."

"Thank you," I said. I made my smile tremble. God, I was so going to hell. Willy picked up my son and left.

I just wanted to get to the end of my pregnancy without a big shake up. Getting involved in crime fighting is how Baby Jude ended up premature. I didn't want the same thing to happen to our princess.

CHAPTER FIVE

*B*abe and Willy took a walk with Jude while Sheriff Taylor sat with me in the living room. I told him about Dracula, Frankenstein's Bride, The Mummy, and the Swamp Monster. He agreed that it all seemed a little too coincidental.

"This invisible man," he said. "Can you tell me anything specific about him? Maybe something that might give us a clue?"

"Uhm, I'm pretty sure the word invisible implies a lack of details."

Sheriff Taylor narrowed his dark eyes at me and gave me a sour look.

"Fine. Sorry." I rolled my eyes. "He considers himself a loner. He's lonely. He's jealous. And he feels like he's been bullied by all the people getting hurt. These pranks, dangerous or not, are his way of getting revenge. He feels like they will see him now."

"You keep saying he." The sheriff nodded. "Are you sure it's a man?"

"No. It's just a feeling. He was jealous of Roger and Karina, but a woman can be jealous too." I felt a little narrow in my thinking to have assumed it was a guy because of the interest in Karina. "It has to be someone who was on the courthouse lawn at the same time as Roger. I know who I saw, but I don't know the workers. It could have been one of them too."

"Now, on Roger, we don't even know if he was pushed. He says it happened too fast, and he doesn't know if he slipped or someone nudged him."

"That's weird. Did he say nudge? Because, if he did, then he was definitely pushed. Do you think he's scared?" I wondered if he thought maybe his girlfriend had given him the "nudge." "Besides," I told the sheriff. "You can't pick and choose what you want to believe in my visions. Either the invisible man did it in all of them, or he did it in none of them."

Sheriff Taylor rubbed his eyes. They were dark around the outside, which was more an indication he was a wereraccoon than an indication of exhaustion. In this case, though, I thought it might be both. "Okay, let's say you're right down the board. The victims are a mixed group. Mark Smart, Evelyn Meyers." He winced when he said his sister-in-law's name. "Roger Parks, and Tyler Thompson." He shrugged. "What do they all have in common?"

"If it weren't for Mark Smart, I'd say they were all assholes to one degree or another."

I got a disapproving look for my observation. "I'm looking for something more substantial."

"You got me, then. I have no idea. Other than the fact that the invisible person feels persecuted by all of them."

"Will you call me if you get any more visions?"

"Sure, but I don't know if it'll do any good." I sagged down, suddenly feeling very grumpy. "I am useless." *Brrrzzzzt.* Oh, joy.

"Did you say something?"

With my butt? "Not hardly."

The sheriff's mouth turned up slightly at the corners as he put his notebook away. *Laugh it up raccoon-boy.* "I best get going. I'll interview everyone and see if I can find something in common. Are you going to the Johnson's Halloween Bash?"

"Princess has made other plans for me." I rubbed my beach-ball belly.

"Well, Jean was hoping to see you. She might stop by to visit you at home if that's okay?"

Jean and I weren't friends exactly, but I found her strangely comforting. I smiled. "I'd like that."

Both Jean and Sheriff Avery were the kind of people I always wished my hippy, tree-hugging parents would have been. "You have a daughter, don't you?"

"Nicole." He smiled fondly. "She's at Stanford working on her Ph.D."

Wow. Stanford was Ivy League and hella expensive. I got a severe case of panic sweat as I thought about what it would cost to send Jude to a place like that, or, jayzus, two kids. "You must be proud," I said. "That's a great college."

41

"She's coming home for Christmas this year. We haven't seen her too much since she graduated with her bachelor's degree in clinical psychology. Her master's and Ph.D. work has kept her a lot busier."

"I'm glad she's coming home."

He leaned forward and touched my hand. "Me too."

BILLY BOB and Chav came over in the evening to check on me again. My blood pressure was almost normal. He also checked my cervix, just in case, which was still thick and hard. I hadn't had any spotting for three weeks, all of which put me on the good list. However, my ankles were just the teensiest bit swollen, so Billy Bob wanted me to increase my exercises to improve my circulation.

"Don't do anything that engages your abdominal wall," Billy Bob warned me.

Bummer. I could have thought of a few things more pleasant than pressing my feet into the bed repetitively, but that was still a no-no as well.

"I get it. Be a turnip." Babe gave my hand a comforting squeeze. I glared at him.

"What?" he asked.

"You did this to me," I said flatly. "This is your fault."

He frowned. "I seem to recall you were complicit in the preceding event."

"Don't be logical. You know I hate it when you get all rational and crap." Especially since I wasn't sure I had a rational bone left in my body. Maybe my patella, but that was it, and it was about to lose its mind. I couldn't stop the tears now as they leaked down my cheeks. I suddenly went from agitated to despondent. "You don't love me." More irrationality.

"Aww, Sunny. You're being ridiculous."

"I'm ridiculous? Did you just seriously call me ridiculous?"

"We're out," said Chav. She grabbed Billy Bob by the hand. "You two don't kill each other."

When the *happy* couple went home, Babe got down on his knees in front of me. He put his cheek on my belly. "You are loved, little one," he said. "You are wanted. You are a tie for the top three things in my life. You, your brother, and your mom."

"No fair," I murmured, the anger leaving me again. I took a deep breath and let it out. His hair, the color of toasted pecans, as thick as it was, was cool against my hot hands. I ran my fingers through it, massaging his scalp. "I hate being cooped up."

"I know." He rubbed the sides of my belly. "But it won't be for long."

"Unless I get pregnant again." I loved Jude, and I knew I would adore this baby, but two pregnancies so close together had me pretty freaked out. "I'm not sure if my body could take doing this again so soon."

He tilted his chin so he could look up at my face. "Then we'll use birth control."

"I could get my tubes tied."

"Can we think about it?"

I nodded but didn't smile. "Sure." I knew he wanted a large family, and I'd planned to give him one. But I wasn't getting any younger, and having a therian baby was already high risk. The baby moved inside me again.

"I can feel her against my cheek," Babe smiled.

"I'll admit, I might miss the unexpected joy I experience every time I realize I'm growing our child inside me." *Brrrzzzzttt Ssssssssssss.* I would not miss flatulence ruining every pleasant moment.

Babe stood up, pretending like he didn't notice. Good man. "I'm going to check on Jude."

"Do that." It was nice he could ignore my body's breakdown, even if I couldn't.

He forgot the baby monitor was on and started laughing when he got into Jude's room. So much for ignoring.

"I hear you!"

He came back out of the backroom with a broad smile on his face. "The boy's sleeping like a baby."

"I'd expect nothing else. It's exhausting work being that cute."

"No doubt." Babe sat on the couch and pulled me into his arms. "You should probably get some sleep too."

"I'm afraid the invisible man isn't done with his revenge tricks, and there's nothing I can do about it.

"You have to quit stressing, darling," Babe said. "You heard the doc."

"Yeah, I heard him." But was I listening? The invisible

man with all his rage was making my life a horror show. Literally. His anger was escalating. What if his next prank did more than injure someone? I wouldn't be able to forgive myself if something happened, and I could have prevented it.

CHAPTER SIX

One day until Halloween...
I'd spent the better part of the night and most of the morning trying to decipher all my visions to no avail.

A knock on my door startled me. "Mrs. Trimmel," a man said at the door. "It's me. Deputy Farraday."

"Come in, Eldin," I said. "Did you bring food?"

He opened the door, wearing his tan deputy uniform and a big smile on his face, and held out a box of donuts. "I stopped by Becky's Bakery on the way over."

"You are an angel." If he didn't get his wings soon, this would seal the deal. "Glazed twists with cinnamon."

Eldin winked. "Becky insisted once I told her they were for you."

"My day is brighter already."

Selena Messer came out of the back with Jude in her arms. God, I missed taking care of my son. "Hey, El," she said. "How are you doing?"

"Good. Doing good," Eldin replied. "And you? Michael said you all have already booked your honeymoon in Costa Rica. I'm jealous."

She beamed. "I gotta get bikini ready by June."

Selena was dating Farraday's co-worker, Deputy Michael Connelly, a lanky man, skinnier than Farraday. But he was a weresquirrel, and they tended to be wiry. It still astounded me when I thought about the tall, curvy bear shifter dating a squirrel. But Selena and Michael were overjoyed. They were planning a June wedding.

I'd seen them together in a psychic reading before they were even on each other's radar.

Gah! I longed for the days of clear and easy to figure out visions.

"Selena's on Sunny duty today, I'm afraid." I cast her a sympathetic look. "I hate that I'm making so much work for everyone."

"Never you mind, Sunny," Selena said. "We Peculiar folk know how to rally around one of our own."

"Indeed," Eldin added with a smile.

Now I wanted to cry again. I was one of their own.

"This boy's a hungry little howler," Selena teased. Jude giggled when she poked his belly and took him into the kitchen.

Eldin took a seat in the chair next to the couch. He pulled a notebook and pencil from his breast pocket. It was similar to the sheriff's. The young man was always so serious about his work. "I have a list of people we've identified as witnesses to each of the incidences. Sheriff Taylor asked me to go through them with you to see if any of them will get your," he waved the pencil at me like a wand, "thing happening."

"I'm not a wizard at Hogwarts," I said, though I thought I could give Hagrid a run for his money in the size department. "It's a psychic ability. I'm clairvoyant, not magical."

"Uh-hm." He nodded and tapped his notepad. "The list."

"Yes, go ahead." I sighed and moved over to the other side of the couch. The poor cushions were taking a beating from my wide ass, and I switched it up every hour in hopes the deep indentions wouldn't become permanent.

"Okay, so with Smart Funeral home, there is the Smart Family, Mark and Judith, along with their children, Jackson, Liberty, and Marianne. They'd had a funeral the day before for Donald Franks."

"I don't think I know him."

"He was one-hundred and eighty-seven. He lived in the Silver Fox Senior Center. He and his wife, deceased thirty years ago, never had any children, so he was pretty much alone."

"Oh." I knew were the center was located, but I'd never been in it. Poor man. "How awful to be in an old folk's home with no one to visit."

"Yeah. If it weren't for the high school volunteers, he wouldn't have had any visitors except for the staff."

"How sad is that?"

"The funeral had a good showing. Thirty-four people from town." He handed me his pad.

I recognized a few names, like Ruth, Ed, and all her kids except Tyler. Posie and Kyle Avery. Posie, Kyle's mom, owned the pawn shop in town now. Beatie and Leonard Parks, those were Roger Park's grandparents. Brady and Jo Jo Corman. Blondina and Roger Messer, along with their kids Selena, Brandon, and Rudy. Also in attendance was, Evelyn Meyers, Jean and Sid Taylor, Michael Connelly, and Eldin. The rest of the names were unfamiliar, and none of the one's I recognized were hitting any notes for me.

"Nada," I said.

"Okay." He took the pad back and smirked. "There were no witnesses to the incident with Evelyn Meyer's car."

"Couldn't have happened to a nicer woman," I said.

"That's about right." He had a twinkle in his eyes. "Moving on. The Park's incident included Kyle Avery, Karina Wells, Selena, Brandon, Jackson, Michele Thompson, Taylor Thompson, Brady Corman, Jo Jo Corman, Larry Michaels, Kevin Smith, and Tommy Brown. The last three were the heavy equipment operators."

"I didn't see Jo Jo."

"He came just as Roger fell into the dig site."

"Oh, and Mayor Trimmel and yourself."

"Yes, of course. What about the old guy?"

"Who?"

It didn't really matter. The man had disappeared by the time I'd crossed the street. Was there any witness to Tyler's incident?"

Eldin's eyes held a brief flash of anger. When I gave

him a questioning glance, he made them carefully neutral. "An anonymous tip sent him there. We were told there was an animal trapped in the cesspit. Tyler was the closest, so he was first on the scene. When he went inside to assess the situation, a black snake fell onto his shoulders, and then there was an explosion. He didn't remember anything else."

"Any witnesses?"

"None."

"How's Tyler doing?"

"Burns are healing, thanks to the doc. Other than that, same as always."

"I guess the explosion didn't knock the asshole out of him, huh?"

Eldin gave me a small smile. "That's no lie, Ma'am."

I guess I wasn't the only one Tyler rubbed the wrong way. "Is there more?" I grabbed a cinnamon twist and bit off the soft, chewy, and scrumptious end. "Mmmmm."

"That's it for now." He stood up. "Do you need anything before I go?"

"No. Thank you, Eldin, and thank Sheriff Taylor for me."

"You are the one owed a thanks, Mrs. Trimmel."

"You know you can call me Sunny, right?" I told him, and not for the first time.

He smiled. "I know. You have a good day, Ma'am."

"Thanks for the donuts."

Selena came out of the kitchen with Jude a few minutes after Farraday left.

I lifted the donut box. "Want one?"

"Sure..." She hesitated. "Better not. I need to lose a couple of pounds. It's been a long time since I've worn a bathing suit."

"Mamamama." Jude clenched and unclenched his hands toward me. I held out my arms and Selena gave him to me.

"How's my good boy?" He made a squealing noise then sprouted fur all over his body and wiggled out of my hands. He'd changed into a coyote pup. His most mobile form.

Selena laughed. The pup was still wearing a pair of shorts and a T-shirt that read, *Moms Rule, Dads Drool*. "I'll take him outside to let him run if you want. I think he's got a lot of pent up energy."

"That's a good idea." I walked with her to the door, and when she opened it, Jude sprinted past out into the grass and began running in circles.

"Energy is wasted on the young," she said.

I looked at her. Selena was in her mid-twenties, a little younger than Babe. "You're still plenty young." I patted her arm. "And perfect just the way you are..."

A song plays in the background. It annoyingly goes on and on about a graveyard smash with monsters as the main guests. The mummy, who has always been a tormenter, is here, so is Dracula, who won't let me go, Frankenstein's bride, who humiliated me in public, the Swamp Man, who is always belittling people, and the phantom, who thinks he's better than everyone else. All of the invisible man's targets in one area. Here's my chance to get them. To make them pay once and for all.

The area goes bright with blazing hot light. A howl startles me, and I see the Wolfman as the flames consume him.

I scream.

"Fire!"

Selena had her arms around me, holding me off the floor. "Sunny, are you all right?"

"No," I told her. "I saw the Wolfman die in the blaze."

CHAPTER SEVEN

All Hallow's Eve...again.

Chavvah brought me some colorful clothes and a scarf to wrap my hair. Ruth had a wig from one of Michele's high school plays. It was a buttery yellow with curls that would make *Annie* jealous. Ruth's younger daughter Dakota put my make-up on. By the time she was done, you couldn't see a trace of the acne. That girl was magic with a concealer wand. I was properly tarted up with dark eye shadow, red lips, and thick eyelashes fluttering like butterfly wings...mostly because I wasn't used to wearing them and I couldn't stop blinking.

Ruth had engaged the Johnson twins to build me a fortune teller booth out of some two-by-fours and plywood, and while they mock grumbled, they happily obliged.

Me sitting for the entire evening was the only way Billy Bob would approve me going.

I did not, however, tell anyone about the vision. I

mean, Selena knew, but I asked her to keep it quiet until I could talk to Babe and the sheriff. I just hadn't told her when I would speak to them.

My nickel jar filled up fast as party-goers kept dropping money in to have their fortunes read. It was good news, all of it, mostly because it was all made-up. My visions weren't working right now, so I kept my answers happy and vague.

Delbert Johnson brought me some punch. "Don't you go having that baby in my barn tonight, Sunny. I know how you like an unconventional birth."

"Har har," I said. "I have no plans to have this kid for at least another month, and in the way nature intended it, on a birthing table in Billy Bob's clinic."

Elbert who'd walked up on the conversation, said, "Good, because Babe ain't Joseph and your baby isn't the Messiah. Which means, there's no room at the inn or in the manger."

"Well, I don't see any wisemen either, just a couple of donkeys, so I think we're safe tonight."

Delbert's light blue eyes twinkled when he smiled. "That's my girl." He winked as he and Elbert left my stand.

Willy Boden sashayed over in an Elvira outfit that put the *voom* in *vava voom*. "Snazzy," I told her. "You look hot as the queen of the night."

"Thanks, Madame Sunshine." She winked. "I'm glad I came down for the party. It's so peaceful in this town. Not like in the city. I feel like I can't even hear myself think anymore when I'm up there."

The music was playing, people were laughing and chatting, and there were haunted house noises going off every few minutes. In other words, there was nothing peaceful about tonight, but I knew what she meant. Moving from San Diego to Peculiar had been a huge shock to the system in a really great way. I wouldn't exchange country living for a big city ever.

Brady and Jo Jo walked in. Brady was dressed as a vampire. I wasn't sure what Jo Jo was going for. He was wearing all leather with fake scars on his arms and a sword on his side. He wore a long wig and had let his scruff grow out a little on his face.

"Damn, he's hot," Willy said.

"He's nineteen years-old," I cautioned her.

She rolled her eyes. "I'm talking about the vamp, not the *Underworld* wannabe."

Oh. She meant Brady. "You should go talk to him."

She smiled. "You think?" Willy looked uncertain of herself, which seemed strange since she was usually full of bravado and confidence. "The last time we spoke, he practically bit my head off."

I didn't even know she'd met Brady before. More and more interesting. "How do you know Brady?"

"When his son disappeared, I came in to help."

That night. The same night the serial killer used me as bait to lure Chavvah out. "Ah. Well, he was probably trying not to drink."

Willy gave me a sharp look. "He said something similar." She tapped the dimple in her chin. "Maybe I'll just go say hi."

I smiled. "You do that."

I kept my eye out for the monsters. I saw Roger,

Evelyn, and Mark, but no Tyler. As long as he wasn't here, people were safe, right? Maybe because of his burns, he wouldn't show up. Ruth had told me he was already home, though, and that he was eager to get back to work.

Voices raised, and not in a celebratory way. I heard Evelyn Meyers say, "I know you had something to do with it, Sid. You and Jean are out to get me."

Paranoid much?

Jean blushed with hot embarrassment, and I thought Sheriff Taylor was going to burst a blood vessel in his forehead. "You are the only one holding a grudge, Evie," Sheriff Taylor said. "You need to watch it."

"Or what? You'll put more crap on my car?" She snapped her fingers at him and hissed, her raccoon side coming out. "I'll make you pay. I swear it."

I saw the old man again. The one from the courthouse lawn. He stared daggers at Evelyn, and I seconded the feeling. That woman was a menace to her family and this town.

Jackson Smart stood nearby, sipping from a punch cup. The other kids his age were standing nearby, but they were talking around him, not to him. Roger and Karina were paired off. Kyle and Michele. Ugh. I hoped Ruth could nip that in the bud. Ever since she and Jo Jo had broken up, she'd been hanging out with that delinquent.

Jo Jo, like Jackson, stood off on his own. But not for long. Soon, a beautiful blonde Little Bo Peep was flirting with him. It made my heart happy. I loved that kid like a brother, and I wanted nothing but wonderful things in his life. I'd been able to give him a message from his mother before her spirit moved on, and the act had bonded me to him. I had to look out for him. I'd promised Rose Ann.

Mark Smart, who was not dressed up at all, *spoil sport*, walked over to Jackson and put his arm around his son's shoulders. Jackson moved a little away from him. Aww. I felt sorry for Mark. His son would be heading off to college soon. I didn't even want to imagine what it would be like when Jude left the nest.

Babe, who was dressed like Thor, yummy yummy, strolled over like a mutherfluffin' superhero.

"Is that a hammer in your pocket or are you just happy to see me?"

He grinned. "I'm always happy to see you, darlin'." He stooped down and kissed me like he meant it. *Yowza*.

"Not fair," I said a bit breathlessly.

"All's fair in love, my beautiful gypsy."

God, I love this man. "When I finally pop this kid out and my six weeks of post-partum crap is done, I am going to lock you in a room and do you until we are both comatose."

Babe laughed. "I could use a good coma vacation."

The old man from earlier sat on a hay bale behind Roger and Karina. "Who is that?" I asked. I pointed where he was sitting.

"Roger Parks," Babe said. "Are you feeling okay?"

"Not him. The old guy behind him."

Babe looked to where I indicated.

"He's sitting on the bale of hay next to the candle."

"I don't see anyone, Sunny. Are you sure you're feeling okay?" He put his hand on my forehead. "You don't feel hot, but I'm going to get the doc, anyhow. I'll be right back."

Babe didn't see him. How could he not... Oh boy. The last time I was seeing things that nobody else could was when I was haunted by my deceased brother-in-law. Could the old guy be a ghost? I could only see shifter ghosts, after all. And I hadn't seen one since the night I helped eight people cross into the light. It had been a traumatic night all around.

I got up and started walking toward the old man. I wanted to talk to him. If he was who I suspected he was, then maybe I could help him not to hurt anyone else.

"Hello," I said.

He ignored me as if I weren't there.

I tried again. "Hey. Are you Donald Franks?"

His head snapped toward me when he heard his name. "Who are you?"

"I'm Sunny."

"I've heard of you." He waved his hand. "Can you see me?"

Crap. I'd found my invisible man. "Yes. I see you, Mr. Franks. I do."

He pointed to Jackson. "They don't see him. He's a good kid. He came in every week to read to me those last couple of months. He deserves better. I can feel his loneliness. His anger. He needs my help to show them."

"To show them what?"

"To show them they can't push him around." The old man shook his head. "I was ready to go, but at my funeral, each of them went out of their way to make him feel small." He shook his gnarled fist at Mark. "He makes Jackson feel like he can never leave Peculiar." He gestured to Evelyn next. "She talked to him like he was lower than pond scum." The ghost glared at Roger. "He treats Jackson like his personal lap dog. They can't get away with it. I won't let them. And that cop," the ghost spat, but nothing landed, thank heavens, "he just shoved Jackson out of the way at the courthouse like he wasn't even there."

I hadn't noticed Chavvah walk up. "Who are you talking to, Sunny? Billy Bob went up to the Johnson house to help Delbert bring down a couple more bags of ice. Babe is on his way to get him. He asked me to sit with you until he gets back."

"Donald Franks' ghost is keeping me company," I said.

"Who?"

Franks gave her a sharp look. Great.

"You're hurting his feelings. He just passed away last week."

"Oh." Chav was dressed as Princess Leia, with the curled buns on both sides of her head and everything.

"You look great by the way."

"Thanks," she said, her tone worried. "You too."

Babe and Billy Bob quickly moved through the crowd toward us. Billy Bob was dressed as Hans Solo.

"I've disappeared again, haven't I?" the ghost asked.

"I still see you, Donald."

"No one called me Donald. It was Donnie. I was always Donnie."

I remembered his wife had passed away thirty years before him. "Aren't you ready to see your loved ones?"

"Soon." He smiled. The *Monster Mash* began to blare through the speakers. The party crowd sent up a cheer.

"Oh no." Heat crept up my body. I felt a pain in my side. A cramp? No. Not this. I tried to stand, but it was difficult.

"Sunny!" Babe's voice was sharp with alarm.

"Get everyone out," I said through clenched teeth. "I can't stop him."

Tyler Thompson came into the barn just as I heard the lyrics "graveyard smash." "The Wolfman," I panted. "Have to get them all out."

The hay bales caught on fire, and the blaze rose unnaturally quick. There was screaming and shoving as people tried to get out of the barn. The dry straw was going up like kindling.

On our way out, Brady was running in, Willy on his heels. "Where's Jo Jo?"

"I..." *Underworld.* The leather outfit. Jo Jo wasn't a vampire. He was a werewolf. In the vision, the invisible man hadn't meant to hurt *the wolfman, but sometimes innocent people got caught in the crossfire. Or in this case, fire-fire.* "I saw him with Little Bo Peep in the back. You have to get him. Save him." I moaned as another cramp pinched my middle. No, no, no. I wasn't having this baby now. Not here. Not in chaos. Not again!

"Jolon!" Brady bellowed. Like the king and queen of the night, Brady and Willy raced toward the back of the barn.

Babe, the doc, and Chav practically carried me out the front. I couldn't breathe as panic welled inside me. The pain was getting worse, and Jo Jo, Willy, Bo Peep, and

Brady still hadn't come out. Most of the guests were pulling water in buckets from the Johnson's well and trying to put out the bales of hay, but the fire seemed to keep one step ahead of them.

"Get me Jackson Smart!"

My husband looked at me like I was nuts.

"Do it!" I said, sounding like the demonically possessed girl from the *Exorcist*. Chav put her arm around me to steady me as Babe went to get the boy.

When he came back with him, Jackson looked as freaked out as the rest of the guests. His face was red with stress, making his white hair even whiter. "You have to make him stop," I told the kid.

"I... Who?"

"Oooooo." Another pain hit and I had to wait for it to ease. "Donald Franks."

"He's dead."

"I know." Gah! Explaining sucked. "His ghost is avenging you on people who treat you bad. I need you to tell him to stop." I pointed to where Franks stood just outside the barn doors, his arms crossed as he kept the fire going despite everyone's efforts.

His father Mark was at his elbow. "Mrs. Trimmel can see the dead, son. I was there the last time she did it. She helped a lot of people that day. If she says she sees a ghost, you must believe her."

I wanted to high-five Mark for believing me without me having to dance through a bunch of hoops, but instead I cried. I couldn't stop the tears. "Babe, I need to go to Franks. Help me. Jackson, you come with us."

Babe and Jackson took me to where I told them that the ghost stood. "Donald Franks," I said. "I've brought Jackson with me. He wants to talk to you."

The ghost turned his attention to me, and the fire in the barn dimmed. "I'm doing this for him." Donald Franks had passed revenge and went right into delusional.

"He knows. But all the people you want to harm are no longer in the barn. Do you really want to take innocent lives? Jackson doesn't want that." I nudged Jackson. "Tell him to stop. You don't need him to fight your battles. Tell him this isn't what you want."

"I'm okay," Jackson said, not sounding at all convinced. "You can stop now."

"I wished we could have finished *Gulliver's Travels*," Franks said.

"He says he would have liked to have heard the end of Gulliver's Travels," I relayed.

Jackson blanched. "Christ, he is here."

"I told you that." I couldn't keep the annoyance out of my tone, but when the ghost turned his vengeful eyes towards me, I said, "He doesn't want to see you picked on and ignored. He's worried people won't see you. The way they didn't see him."

"Mr. Franks. I have family that loves me, and I have good friends, even if it doesn't seem like it. I don't want you to hurt anyone. Not for me. Please stop."

Franks narrowed his eyes. "I don't believe him."

"He needs more convincing." The shouts of people fighting the fire were getting louder. "Convince him."

"I love my dad. I'd never want to see him hurt. Ms.

Meyers, Roger, and Tyler Thompson don't mean anything in my life. If you hurt them, you are doing it for yourself, not for me. You were a nice man. Kind. You told me once that you met your wife on a hunger mission. Don't do this. Don't be a man she wouldn't have wanted to know."

The ghost's face crumpled. He wailed with agony at Jackson's words. The flames in the barn shot straight up into the air and then extinguished.

The ghost vanished.

"I felt that," Jackson said. "It was like air and light."

Babe hugged me close to his chest. "You did it, Sunny."

"Jo Jo?" Had I been too late? My question was answered as Willy and Brady brought out Jo Jo and his date. They were coughing up a storm, but at least they were walking on their own. "Thank heavens." I grabbed Babe's Thor cape and blew my nose.

"You are so sexy right now," he said.

"Shut up."

"Are you still having pain?"

I stopped for a moment and assessed. Nope. The pain was gone. "I'm fine now. False alarm."

I could feel the tension drain from my man as he squeezed me so tight... *Brrrzzzttttbhhssssss. Brrrsss. Sssss.*

CHAPTER EIGHT

Three weeks later...Thanksgiving.
I sat up in bed. My stomach still ached from a long night in the delivery room. Billy Bob came into the room and handed our daughter to Babe.

"She's so beautiful," Babe said. He swallowed as he gazed upon her face. "A ray of sunshine, just like her mama."

Chavvah got in on the auntie action. "She really is gorgeous." Chav smiled at me.

"We're not naming her Sunny," I said. "Give me my baby."

Babe and Chav chuckled, but they handed her over. My gosh, the sun really did shine from her. "What do you think of Dawn?"

"Because with Dawn comes the sun," Babe said. "I think it fits. What about a middle name?"

"Adine, I think." I looked over at my best friend. Adine

was Chavvah's middle name. In Hebrew it meant tender. I always thought it was lovely. "Dawn Adine Trimmel."

"You're going to make me cry, Sunny."

"Join the club," Ruth said, as she carried Jude into the room. "Happy Thanksgiving, folks."

Ruth had taken Jude when my labor started. I couldn't believe I went into labor with Jude the day before Valentine's Day, and now with Dawn, the day before Thanksgiving. Granted, she wasn't born until this evening. Sixteen hours of labor had pretty much convinced me that an epidural would be on the menu if we had any more children. I couldn't even close my eyes without reliving the pain of those contractions.

At least the horror movie visions went away when Donald Frank moved on. Jackson couldn't believe he'd made such an impact on another person. It's convinced him to continue volunteering at the senior center even though he no longer needed it for a scholarship. Willy went back home to Kansas City after that weekend, but she texted me all the time. I'm betting she'll be back. I think our little bobcat has her eye on a particular coyote.

Evelyn and Roger are still assholes. Have a ghost seeking revenge should have shocked them into acting right. Like when the ghosts visited Scrooge McDuck. But no such luck. If they could have figured out how to press charges against a dead guy, they would have. I had noticed Tyler had been a little less gruff, though. Maybe some good came out of the haunting prankster after all.

Billy Bob came back in the room. "Several people in

town have brought left over Thanksgiving dinner for us. You all want to eat?"

"I'm starved," I said. "Having a baby is hungry work."

Babe kissed me. It was so sweet and gentle. "I love you, Sunny." He kissed our daughter on the forehead. "You did so good."

"Yeah?" I looked down at Dawn. "*We* really did."

The End
Read the next books in the Series!

In The Midnight Howl
(Peculiar Mysteries & Romances Book 5)

Intrigue, murder, and a town full of suspects will

test Wilhelmina "Willy" Boden's investigative skills as an outsider in Peculiar.

*****

When an anonymous whistleblower from Peculiar, Missouri alleges that the mayor's wife is a fraud, the Shifter Tri-State Council decides to send me in to investigate. Problem is, I like the people in this town, and I don't want to betray any of them...especially a certain handsome were-coyote named Brady Corman.

Unfortunately, I don't get paid to make friends or dates.

But when the local pain-in-the-ass aka "the whistle-blower" is found dead, and both the town's beloved Sheriff and Brady's teenaged son are prime suspects, along with half the town, I have to investigate.

As much as I'd like to ignore the evidence, my sense of duty won't let me turn a blind eye to injustice. My loyalty to my friends will be tested and my relationship with Brady may be over before it even begins.

What's a werebobcat to do when my instincts tell her one thing and my heart the exact opposite?

**Furred Lines
(Peculiar Mysteries & Romances Book 6)**

A SERIES of murders across the state sends rookie FBI agent Nicole Taylor to familiar territory—her hometown of Peculiar.

*****

When I am assigned my first case, a dangerous serial killer known as Little Piggy, I am thrilled and excited to put my profiler skills to the test.

I might have an advanced degree in psychology and graduated top of my class at Quantico, but my partner, the oh-so-yummy senior field agent and werebear Dominic Tartan, acts like I'm still in school.

Half the time he acts like he wants to ditch me, the other half of the time I'm pretty sure he wants to kiss me.

He's not the only one struggling. I don't know whether

to sock him one or jump his bones. Most of the time I want to do both.

The case gets personal when Little Piggy takes someone from Peculiar. Dom and I need to put our differences and our hormones aside to catch the supernatural criminal before his latest kidnap victim ends up dead.

Sense and Scent Ability
(A Nora Black Midlife Psychic Mystery Book 1)

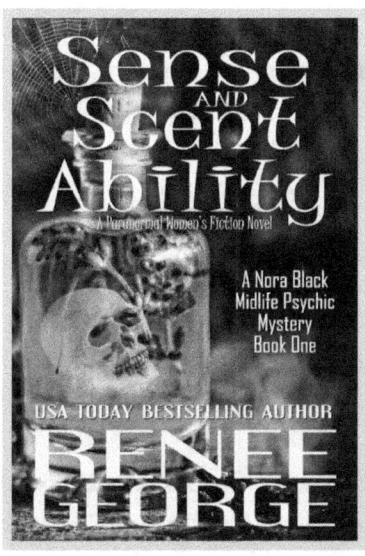

MY NAME IS NORA BLACK, and I'm fifty-one-years young. At least that's what I tell myself, when I'm not having hot flashes, my knees don't hurt, and I can find my reading glasses.

I'm also the proud owner of a salon called Scents &

Scentsability in the small resort town of Garden Cove, where I make a cozy living selling handmade bath and beauty products. All in all, my life's is pretty good.

Except for one little glitch...

Since my recent hysterectomy, where I died on the operating table, I've been experiencing what some might call paranormal activity. No, I don't see dead people, but quite suddenly I'm triggered by scents that, in their wake, leave behind these vividly intense memories. Sometimes they're unfocused and hazy, but there's no doubt, they are very, very real.

Know what else? They're not my memories. It seems I've lost a uterus and gained a psychic gift.

When my best friend Gilly's abusive boyfriend ends up dead after a fire, and she becomes the prime suspect, I end up a babysitter to her two teenagers while she's locked up in the clink. Add to that my super sniffer's newly acquired abilities and a rash of memories connected to the real criminal, and I find myself in a race to catch a killer before my best friend is tried for murder.

Earth Spells Are Easy
(Grimoires of a Middle-aged Witch Book 1)

AS A FORTY-THREE-YEAR-OLD, newly divorced, single mom, I know two things for certain, starting over sucks, and magic isn't real. At least that's what I thought. I mean, starting over really does stink, but when it comes to magic, I have to rethink everything.

I've spent the last year since my ex left me going through the motions. Get up. Work. Care for a grumpy teenager. Cook dinner. Go to bed. Wash. Rinse. Repeat.

Nothing changes... Until it does.

After bidding on a box of old books at an estate auction, I'm experiencing changes.

And I'm not talking about menopause.

My garden gnome Linda has come to life. No, really. Her name is Linda, and she never shuts up. A chonky cat with a few secrets of his own has adopted me. And a gorgeous professor of the occult tells me I'm a witch.

Right now, I'm not sure who's crazier—me, Linda or the hottie professor.

If this is my new reality, it's nature's cruel midlife trick. I'm learning fast that earth spells might be easy, but they aren't cheap. All magic exacts a toll, and if I don't master the elements, the elements will be the death of me.

Literally.

IN THE MIDNIGHT HOWL - SNEAK PEEK

Peculiar Mysteries Book 5

Chapter One

For more than a year, I had dreamed, no, fantasized about getting back to Peculiar, Missouri. My first visit last June during the Tri-State Council Jubilee had made me fall in love with the town. I'd made friends. Sunny Haddock, who was married to the mayor Babel Trimmel, was funny, sweet and self-deprecating. I could hang out with her all day doing nothing and still have a blast. Chavvah Trimmel, Sunny's best friend and sister-in-law, not to mention all around bad-ass chick, was one of the most solid people I'd ever met. But I think I liked Ruth Thompson the best.

Ruth was the kind of woman, whom on paper, I would never have imagined as a friend. She'd been married more than twenty years, had nine kids, and seemed to know the dirt on everyone in the small community. And last, but certainly not least, on that list of awesome people was sexy, broody Brady Corman. We'd had a moment when I'd been in Peculiar for Halloween, and I'd hoped to take that sizzling connection and turn it into an extended adventure.

But right now, as I avoided the gazes of those people I'd wanted to call friends, I knew whatever chance I'd had to be a part of Peculiar—and part of Brady's life—was gone. As an investigator for the Council, I had a job to do, and I took my oath and duty very seriously. That's why I was here, at this moment, destroying my new friendships.

I turned to Sheriff Taylor and said, "I'm sorry, Sid, you know I don't want to do this."

"It's okay, Willy."

"I have to make it official."

He nodded. "I understand."

"Sheriff Sidney Taylor of Peculiar, Missouri, in accordance with the terms of therianthropic protocol as regulated by the Tri-State Council, I have the authority to relieve you of your duty in this investigation and suspend you from this office until said investigation is resolved." This last part killed me to say. "I'll need your badge and weapon."

Sheriff Taylor, his eyes unnaturally dark, which was saying a lot since he's a raccoon shifter, took his badge from his shirt and placed it on Deputy Farraday's desk. Next, he unholstered his gun and set it down next to the silver star. His gaze scraped across the office at his people, including Deputies Farraday, Connelly, and Thompson. Mayor Babel Trimmel, Sunny, Chavvah, Dr. Smith, Ruth Thompson, the sheriff's wife, Jean, and their daughter, Nicole. There was a rise of protest throughout the group, but Sheriff Taylor raised his hand.

"I stand by what I did," he said, his voice as tired as his eyes. He looked at his daughter. "I'd do it again."

"Dad," she said.

Sheriff Taylor held his head high, stoic in his resignation. "Don't."

"Oh, Sid," Jean said and threw her arms around him. She turned an accusing finger at me. "He trusted you. How could you do this?"

In the face of all the disappointed and angry glares from the gathered crowd, I wanted to relent, tell everyone what a big mistake I made. However, he had hidden evidence in a crucial investigation. His choice. Which is why the Council had pulled rank and forced me into this despicable situation.

Four Days earlier...

"You're here!" Ruth said, standing in the open doorway to her two-story pink house with blue trim. "I've made up Dakota's room for you. She'll be sharing a bed with Michele while you're here."

Yellow and purple flowers lined the concrete walkway leading to her front porch, painting a real pretty picture of rural living. "I don't want to put you through any trouble," I told the enthusiastic deer shifter. "I could have just stayed in the motel."

"Oh, pish-posh. I'll hear none of that. Ed, the kids, and I are happy to have you. Besides, I've baked three pies for your visit, so you have to--"

I waved my hand. "You had me at pie."

Ruth laughed. "Good. Now, let's get your bags inside." I only had one suitcase and a vanity. "I'm so excited to see you again. I'm glad you decided to come down for your vacation."

"I needed a little getaway from the old job," I lied. The fib, and not a little white one, made me feel like shit. I did not want to keep things from Ruth. But telling the truth, in this case, would be so much worse. The Tri-State Council had sent me to Peculiar to investigate a rumor about Sunshine "Sunny" Trimmel. They'd received an anonymous letter from a whistleblower that stated, "The mayor's wife isn't what you think she is. Sunny Trimmel is an imposter." Personally, I didn't care whether Sunny was a marshmallow creature from the moon, she'd become a friend, and I didn't particularly like spying on people I cared about.

Better me than someone else though. At least I would operate under the impression that Sunny was innocent until proven guilty, unlike some of my jackass counterparts. The Tri-State Council had officially praised Peculiar and its police force for solving a several-years-old murder spree. Never the less, the killers had been the president of the Tri-State Council's sons, and while it wasn't Chavvah or Sunny's fault, there had been some misdirected hard feelings toward the pair of friends.

Ruth insisted on taking the larger suitcase, and after the long drive down, I didn't have the energy to argue. Besides, I don't think I'd have won if I'd tried.

I loved Ruth's home. Especially the kitchen. It held a

genuine warmth, a feeling of family. I followed her through the living room to a narrow stairwell, and we traveled up to the second floor.

"Dakota's room is just up on the left here. The door at the end of the hall is the bathroom. What time do you normally get up in the morning?"

"Usually around seven. Why?"

"I'll make sure the kids stay out of there from seven to seven-fifteen." She smiled. "With nine people in the house, even with three bathrooms, one on the second floor, two downstairs, we have to use a system or chaos reigns."

I laughed. "I can see that."

"Here we are," Ruth said brightly. She opened the door.

Her oldest daughter's room was painted a soft rose with a darker pink border decorated in pastel blue swooshes around the ceiling. Her queen-sized bed was covered in a buttercream quilted comforter with royal blue and buttercream throw pillows stacked by the headboard. There was typical fare like pictures of her and her friends attached to a memory board, band posters, and various mementos. The furniture consisted of a rustic white-washed dresser, a matching bedside stand, a vanity with a lighted mirror, and a chair with the seat covered in the same royal blue as the pillows. On the stand, was a lamp with a pink lampshade and a dog-eared copy of Michele Bardsley's *I'm The Vampire, That's Why*. I was a fan of the Broken Heart Vampires, so I approved.

"You in the mood for a little outing?" Ruth said as we hauled my bags into the room.

"What you got in mind?"

"Michele is doing community theater." Ruth's pert nose wrinkled in a way that told me she was hiding something. "I'd like to watch the rehearsal."

"Uhm, sure." I gave her some direct eye contact. "Is there something else?"

"Well..." A small smile tugged at the corners of her lips. "I thought it'd be fun."

"And?"

"And, you know... Oh! Sunny's directing. You'd like to see Sunny, right? You haven't been back since Halloween."

I did want to see Sunny, even with the guilt poking at my gut. "What else?" She was keeping something back.

Ruth scratched her head behind her ear and wiggled her mouth. Finally, after a super heavy sigh, she confessed, "Brady is set building today. I thought you might want to say hello. I mean, you all seemed to get along so well at the Halloween party."

Ugh. The Halloween fiasco. The Johnson's barn went up in flames, and it almost ended in disaster for Brady's son Jo Jo. But that wasn't the fiasco I meant. I'd thought Brady was handsome the first time I saw him last June. A little broken, but that had made him even more irresistible to me. I had a history of picking unavailable or emotionally damaged men. Brady, it turned out, had been a little of both. We'd had a real moment that evening. A connection. Until I kissed him, and he ran off like his tail was on fire.

"I don't think anything will be happening between Brady Corman and myself."

"Well, then don't come for Brady. Come for Sunny. Come for me. I'd love the company."

"As long as you don't play matchmaker."

Ruth grinned. "Deal."

The community center was down on Riverfront Street. It was only five small town blocks from Ruth's house, so we walked. Damn, I loved this town. The sky seemed bluer in Peculiar. The grass greener, the trees lusher, and the air sweeter. I envied the folks who lived here year-round. I lived on the Kansas side of Kansas City in a busy, hectic, noisy neighborhood. It was a short drive to the Tri-State Council offices in Overland Park, which made it convenient for work, but I'd never thought about how much I hated apartment living until I'd spent time in this little town. Now, Peculiar was all I could think about.

"Laertes, you're up," I heard Sunny say with some authority. "Take it from act one, scene two. Claudius says, What would'st thou have, Laertes?"

Eight men and three women crowded the small stage. One of the women, I recognized as Ruth's daughter Michele, one was a plain jane with dark curly hair, and the third, who sat on a crafted throne, had black hair pulled back in a severe bun.

Eldin Farraday, a deputy with the Peculiar Sheriff's Department, stumbled out on stage. His cheeks flushed. "Sorry. Sorry," he said.

The black-haired woman's face pinched with irritation. "This is ridiculous." She stood up and straightened her skirt. "How are we supposed to put on a proper play when half the cast doesn't take it seriously?"

"I take my part plenty serious," Eldin said.

From the back of the community theater, a spotlight pinpointed the woman's face. She threw up her hand to block the blinding light. "What in the blazes?" she exclaimed.

The spotlight went out. I looked back to see Taylor Thompson, one of Ruth's twins, wave his hand. "Sorry. My bad." There was a twinkle of mischief in his eyes.

I liked that young man. I turned back to the stage to study the irritated woman. She reminded me of some of the women who used to flutter around my dad when I was young. He was a leader in our community. Without a mate, he'd become a prime candidate for the vultures who wanted to be his wife for the status alone. They were the kind of creatures who yearned for power, if only on a small scale, and were only happy if everyone else was afraid. This woman worked at breeding fear.

"Now, Evelyn," Sunny said. "We'll get all the kinks worked out before opening night. You just let me worry about the details."

"I'll thank you to mind who you're talking to," Evelyn snapped. "I'm not going to take sass from a--"

"Hello," Ruth shouted. "Look who I have with me!"

Sunny's eyes widened with pleased surprise when she saw me. "Willy!" Her hair was longer and blonder—and hey, she wasn't pregnant for once. She bounded down the aisle to me and clasped me by the shoulders before dragging me into a spine crunching hug.

"Hey, girl." I squeezed her back. Guilt pinched at me, and I brushed it aside. "It's so good to see you." I leaned back to get a better look at her. No bags or dark circles under her eyes. Her figure was back to pre-pregnancy shape, and, for a mom of two babies, she appeared remarkably well-rested. "You look great."

"Thanks," she said. "I feel great. What are you doing back in town? Can't get enough of Peculiar night life?"

I chuckled and hoped it didn't sound as forced as it felt. I nodded toward the stage. "Who's the bitch?"

Sunny didn't even turn around to see who I was looking at. "Evelyn Meyers. The town's conscience."

Ruth snorted. "That's one word for it. I can't believe she and Jean Taylor are sisters. Jean is such a lovely woman.'"

Jean was Sheriff Taylor's wife. I'd gotten to know them on my first trip to Peculiar. I'd even had dinner at their home. Watching Evelyn now, I could see the familial resemblance. "I'd fire her cranky ass," I said.

"I can't," Sunny said. Under her breath, she added, "She's funding the whole thing."

Ruth moved in closer and said in a hushed voice, "How's Michele doing?"

"Why are we whispering?"

"Because I don't want her to think I'm checking up on her."

"But you are," I pointed out.

Sunny giggled. "Michele is killing it as Ophelia," Sunny gushed.

Ruth beamed with pride.

Sunny looked at me, her face going curiously blank for about three seconds. When she animated again, she said, "Brady is backstage building the graveyard set. You should go back and see him."

I gave a quick shake of my head. "Nah. I'm sure I'll see him later." Or maybe not. I mean, I wanted to see him, but I liked myself too much to put myself in a position to get shot down again.

"That's not the line, you ignorant child," Evelyn screeched from the stage. Her well-timed tirade took the Brady heat off me for the moment. I looked past Sunny to see who was getting the brunt of her ire.

Jo Jo stood in front of Evelyn, fists clenched, his face red with anger and embarrassment. "It is the line, Ms. Meyers." He held up his copy of the play. "Unless William Shakespeare wrote more than one version."

Evelyn blanched. "You're fired, Jolon Corman. Fired!"

Jo Jo tossed his script down and stormed off the stage. He stopped when he got to Sunny. "Someday someone is going to put that witch in her place."

"Don't go," Sunny said. "I'll take care of this."

"I can't deal with her today." He shook his head. "I'll go see if Chav needs help with the new guy at the cafe." When Sunny wasn't a play director, mother of two, and wife to the mayor, she ran the vegetarian café she co-owned with Chavvah. Yeah, I know. A vegetarian café in a shifter town was weird, but for Peculiar it worked.

"You'll come back though, Jo Jo? This play needs its Hamlet."

He glared up at the stage, his green eyes flashing with

animosity. "Yeah, I'll be back." He looked at Sunny. "But for you, not for her."

After he had left, Sunny sashayed down the aisle, a bright smile on her face. "You can't fire Jo Jo," she told the older woman.

"Should we go help?" I asked.

Ruth shook her head. "Sunny can handle Evelyn."

"I'm paying for this play." Meyers stood up and crossed her arms. "I can fire who I want."

Sunny's whole body stilled. She walked up the four steps to the stage. With her hands on her hips, she smiled even bigger at Evelyn who had sat back down on her makeshift throne. "While it might be difficult, I'm certain I can find someone else to play Queen Gertrude if your choice is to pull your money and leave." She looked over her shoulder. "Hey, Ruth, how do you feel about Shakespeare?"

"Jo Jo can stay," interrupted Evelyn. She sniffed. "So long as he gets his lines right from now on."

Sunny's smile turned nearly feral. "If you get the urge to fire anyone else, Evelyn, you'll be doing this play alone."

The cast on stage all nodded, silently agreeing to walk out with Sunny.

"I'm scared of her," I told Ruth. "She's fierce."

"Sunny's very good with people." Ruth wrinkled her nose. "Why do you think we asked her to be the director? She has a gift."

A gift I was sent to uncover. What had anonymous meant when they'd written, "She's not one of us." The way most of the community loved and defended Sunny, I'd say there wasn't anyone who was one of them more than the blonde wonder.

"Hey, Sunny. Do you want the gravesite on wheels or furniture slides?" a deep, rough voice asked.

It froze me in place. Brady Corman walked out from behind the curtain, all six-foot, sexy-as-hell, melt-my-panties coyote shifter. Wow. I honest to goodness swooned. I waited for him to notice me. It took all of about two seconds.

"Uhm, I'll figure it out," he told Sunny and escaped back behind the curtains.

His reaction, or lack thereof, disappointed me. "This is ridiculous."

"I'm sorry, Willy." Ruth put her hand on my shoulder. "I just thought... Oh, well. It's nothing a little sweet tea, apple pie, and some good company can't fix." She whistled up at the stage. "You all wrapping this up soon? Maybe Chavvah can take a break and join us?"

"Sure, that's probably a good idea, considering." Sunny gave Evelyn a pointed look. The woman's expression soured even more. I got the feeling Evelyn didn't like people who stood up to her. Sunny circled her finger. "Let's take a break and meet back here at four to rehearse Act One Scene Two, which means I'll need Evelyn, Milo, Roger, Michele, Eldin, and Sabrina to come back. I'll message Jo Jo, Billy Bob, and Elton. The first scene is nailed, but the second scene is a hot mess."

"Because some people don't take it seriously," Evelyn said. Sunny pivoted to glare at the woman. Evelyn shut up, even though her face still looked like she was sucking on lemons.

"When are they putting this play on?" I asked Ruth out the side of my mouth.

"In eight weeks," she whispered.

"How long have they been rehearsing?"

"Three weeks."

"I'm afraid two months isn't going to be enough time."

Ruth smiled. "Sunny will get them there."

"You have a lot of faith in her, don't you?"

"She's one of the most genuine people I know," Ruth said.

That's not what the anonymous letter had said. "How long has she been in Peculiar?"

"About two years now."

"And was she an integrator, or is she from another therian community?"

Ruth hesitated, then said, "Uhm, she lived in San Diego before here."

"So, integrator?" Integrators were therianthropes who lived in human populated areas and hid their real selves from everyone around them. Technically, I was an integrator now since going to work for the Council, but my dad had raised my brother and me in a small therian town in southern Kansas near Oklahoma.

"Sure," Ruth said a little too brightly. She blinked then lightly smacked her forehead with her palm. "Oh, shoot. I'm supposed to pick up Linus from his summer camp. I don't know what's going on with the boy, but he can get a little dramatic if I'm late."

I snorted. "My brother once cried because I got one more marshmallow in my bowl of cereal than he did. Believe me, I know dramatic." My younger brother Hans is needy, which is just a nice way of saying he's a big fucking baby. "You get on out of here and get him, I'll meet you over at Sunny's Outlook when you get back."

While Sunny gave last minute orders to her cast, Eldin Farraday made his way down to me. His gray-green eyes made his ordinary face memorable. He was tall, thin, and handsome, and close to my age, and to top it off, he was a really good deputy. He'd been instrumental in taking down the Lowry brothers last June. Why couldn't I fall for a guy like that? Sweet, uncomplicated, and reliable.

"Hey, Willy," Eldin said. "Nice to see you back in town."

"It's nice to be seen." I smiled. "Laertes, huh? You know he buys it in the last act."

"Now you went and ruined the whole play for me." Eldin chortled, an easy laugh, his eyes crinkling at the edges. "And here I thought I was playing the hero."

"Well, they don't call the play Laertes, do they?" I laughed. He really was a nice man. "You want to come over to Sunny's Outlook for some lunch with Sunny and me?"

A throat cleared behind me. Eldin's face brightened. Taylor Thompson, the thinner of Ruth's oldest boys, raised his brow at the deputy. I nearly got burned from the sparks arcing between the two. Well, that was that. I checked Eldin Farraday off my list of eligible bachelors.

Eldin smiled at me. "Sorry, Willy. I've got plans. Maybe another time."

"You got it," I said. As the two men walked out of the

community center, I felt a small pang of jealousy. How awesome would it be for Brady to look at me like that?

The next thing I knew Evelyn Meyers stood next to me, her arms crossed over her chest. "Those two should be ashamed." The unpleasant woman was a few inches taller than me, no big shocker. I was usually the shortest girl in a room of therians. "It's unnatural."

"Oh, c'mon," I said. "A deputy dating a civilian isn't against the law."

She gaped at me. "Are you seriously that dense?"

I took a tool from Sunny's people-skills bag and smiled widely. "Don't you find intolerance more unnatural? I'd rather be around two dudes in love than someone bitter and judgmental."

Evelyn glared at me. "I know why you're here, Ms. Boden. You'll be better served by doing your job and keeping your opinions to yourself."

Same to you, honey.

She stomped off, muttering under her breath.

Sunny joined me as I watched Evelyn go.

"That woman needs to get laid," said Sunny.

I choked on a laugh. "She needs something." One thing was certain, I might not know Sunny's secret, but Evelyn Meyers probably did. My heart sunk at the thought of that awful woman being whistleblower. I'd have to have a private chat with the wicked witch of Peculiar, and soon.

Available at All Your Favorite eTailers

ABOUT THE AUTHOR

I am a USA Today Bestselling author who writes paranormal mysteries and romances because I love all things whodunit, Otherworldly, and weird. Also, I wish my pittie, the adorable Kona Princess Warrior and my two cats Ash and Simon could talk. Or at least be more like Scooby-Doo and help me unmask villains at the haunted house up the street.

When I'm not writing about mystery-solving were-cougars or the adventures of a hapless psychic living among shapeshifters, I am preyed upon by stray kittens who end up living in my house because I can't say no to those sweet, furry faces. (Someone stop telling them where I live!)

I live in Mid-Missouri with my family and I spend my non-writing time doing really cool stuff...like watching TV and cleaning up dog poop

Follow Renee!
Bookbub
Renee's Rebel Readers FB Group
Newsletter